On Two Worlds

Spiritual, Healing, and Unusual Dreams

By: Dr. Saul Shaye

ABOUT THE HEALER

"Inspirational; A genuine Healer."

V. Crystal
Registered Nurse
Brisbane, Austrailia

"Gave me trust in the healing powers in the Universe. Very Inspiring."

E. Van Pragg
Psychologist
Amsterdam, Holland

"Immensely stimulating and inspiring. Demonstration most convincing."

E. Grindley
Radionic Practitioner
Findhorn Foundation
Scotland

"Remarkable technique for channeling, realigning and healing body without touching."

D. Surman
Business Consultant
London, England

"Totally Fantastic."

J. Evans
M. Kline
A.R.E. Representatives
San Diego, California

ABOUT THE HEALER

The response from the private healing sessions has been very positive. One man, who suffered ongoing pain from a past auto accident, has had much relief. Not only has the pain lessened significantly but toes of a foot, which had been damaged in the accident, are beginning to return to their normal position - after he had been told nothing would be done. My husband's back is better than it has been in years, even our dog, who you were so kind to do a healing on has greatly improved. He has no connecting tissue between the joint of his left ankle. For weeks after the healing, he was running and playing like I have never seen him do.

Pat Carpenter
Unity Church of Vermont

"One of the few authentic healers in the world today."

Sasha White, Chair & C.E.O.
Campaign for the Earth Foundation

ABOUT THE DREAMER

"Dr. Saul Shaye is known to hundreds of people, whose lives he has touched, as the "Dream man." He has remembered over 15,000 dream experiences, during which he has received deep spiritual insight and guidance, which he has been able to apply in healing. By bridging higher and lower realms of consciousness, he has shown the ability to connect with ancient knowledge and wisdom."

Nancy Love (President)
National Federation of
Spiritual Healers of America

"Dr. Saul Shaye is a professional of the highest quality. He is loving, sincere, and especially gifted with knowledge he received during dream states. Unlike most of us who dream and forget, Dr. Shaye has phenomenal recall and is able to apply the information. He is an inspiring speaker and healer, working with unconditional love."

Audrey Murr Copland
International Representative
National Federation of Spiritual
Healers of the United Kingdom
INT. REP. NFSHA, INC.

This book is published in the United States of America, & manufactured by Southern Graphics, West Monroe, Louisiana.

Cover Art and Illustrations by Glen M. McCulley.

First Printing - November 1992
Second Printing - September 1995
Third Printing - June 2001
EBSCO Media
Birmingham, Alabama

TABLE OF CONTENTS

VII. CHAPTER SIX (UNUSUAL DREAMS)

VIII. CHAPTER SEVEN

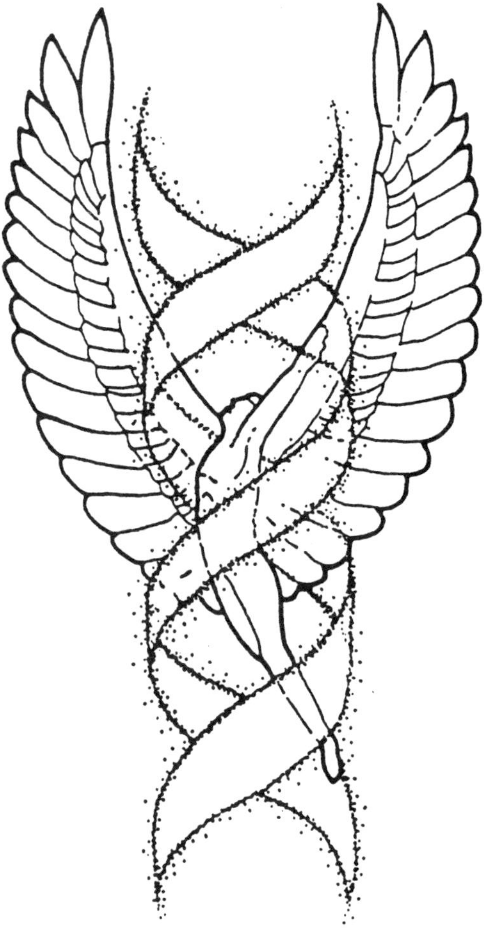

UNIVERSAL HOLISTIC HEALERS ASSOCIATION

PROLOGUE

Unlike the average person, I pay attention to my dreams. I believe that dreams are messages from the super and subconscious mind and use them as sound advice. A person's dreams are his own individual symbolism. Others can help one to understand the symbols, but only the dreamer can know the exact meaning of his or her own dream. In one of my dreams, someone asked, "Are you the dream man?" My answer was, "Yes," and with good reason. Since 1975, I have recorded over 15,000 of my own dreams and have chronicled many of them in a journal. The amazing number of dreams I am able to remember makes me feel that I'm two different people. One "Self" travels the universe by night visiting exotic places, seeing other worlds and talking with famous people (Past and Present) in something called a dream. The other (Self) puts on a white coat during the day and acts out the role of chiropractor in something called a physical body. After giving a workshop in North Carolina recently, a person slipped a note into my hands with six words written on it that summarize my life today. The note read, "He who walks on two worlds."

When I first began developing my "Dream Self", it was pointed out to me that when facing an important decision or problem,I should write out a question on a pad and place it beside my bed. I was told that the answer would soon appear in the form of a dream. One of my first attempts at this exercise gave me a very specific answer. I had a question: "Should I write?" I had a dream: "I was in a gunfight in the old west. My opponent reached for his pistols in his holsters. I reached for my holsters and drew out two pencils and shot him before he could shoot me." I decided I should write!

Another dream told me where to live. My question was: "Should I move?" This is what I dreamed: "I was a very tiny baby in a crib who couldn't move. A baby in another crib was able to move because he was bigger." The dream told me that I should stay where I was for the time being.

In 1976, I put this question to the test: "Is Chiropractic the correct path for me?" This dream followed: "There were upheavals and destruction all around. I said, I'm glad I'm a chiropractor, because all I need is my hands. I knew that I had chosen the correct profession."

Dreams have given me advice, answers and confirmation on numerous topics and have become as much a part of my memory as events that I have physically experienced. I've even relived them in further dreams.

I have put together about one hundred of my favorite dreams and have loosely placed them in categories such as: Spiritual; Healing: Visionary;

Easy To Apply; Edgar Cayce and Unusual Dreams. The language of the dreams may seem difficult to understand in some instances. I have tried to keep the wording of the dreams as similar to the way it was recorded as possible, but I have touched up certain portions for clarity. I didn't want to change the english of the dream (subconscious mind) to the english of the conscious mind, as I thought too much of the dream's original meaning might be lost in the translation.

I am not posing as a dream expert in this book, but, instead, a person who dreams a lot with frequent dream recall. Another factor that separates me from the ordinary dreamer is that my dreams seem to tell an ongoing story. I have received a great deal of insight and beneficial guidance from my dreams, and it is my intention to present this without a lot of philosophy or psychology. I'll leave that to those who wish to generalize with universal symbols and Freudian explanations. I hope you enjoy this selection of dreams and use them to awaken your own "Dream Man" within.

A number of years ago, my brother, Norman, made this statement after I told him about some of my more dramatic visionary and spiritual dreams: "Saul, either you are going to be quite famous someday or else you're going to need a lot of psychiatric treatment." I do hope it's the former.

Chapter One

INTRODUCTION TO SPIRITUAL DREAMS

Although my life consists of two worlds today, there was a time that it didn't. I grew up in Brooklyn, New York, in a semi-orthodox, Jewish household. We followed the traditions of our culture by going to temple on holidays, but God or Spirit was never mentioned. I saw nothing of spirituality in my ghetto home and only violence and cruelty on the streets of Brownsville and Williamburgh, where I spent most of my youth. I remained an Atheist throughout my childhood, even through a near fatal motorcycle accident in 1967.

That accident occurred on a cold, rainy November evening, shortly after I left the Brooklyn college library and began my journey home. Because of the misty rain, I put on a face visor, which worsened visibility, and a thick fog added to the problem. About one mile from home, an unlit, disabled trailer truck suddenly appeared on the road directly in front of me. Before I could do anything to avoid hitting the huge truck, I crashed into it. A split second later, I found myself on the ground in excruciating pain, disoriented and coughing up blood to the extent that I thought I was dying. All I could think of at the time was that life seemed so meaningless. I was twenty years old and hadn't done anything that mattered; now it was about to end.

In retrospect, that was when spirit began to reveal itself in my life. I was at my lowest point, ready to die and feeling that life was a waste. There couldn't have been a better time for spirit to show me that life not only mattered, but that God had special plans for me.

About an hour after the accident, an ambulance finally arrived. When I got to the hospital, I waited another three hours in the emergency room before a doctor examined me. He cleaned off the dried blood, x-rayed the chest, then told me the unbelievable truth. He said that, other than some torn muscles and a lacerated, swollen lower leg and knee, there was no new bleeding and my injuries were minor. I was quite astonished at his prognosis, but elated to know that I was being given another chance at living. At 3:00A.M., I left the hospital on crutches with stitches in my knee and with new determination to make some changes in my world.

That accident marked the end of those early years and closed the door to a Saul Shaye that is merely a memory and somewhat of a mystery as well. From that moment on, my life began to change.

Two months after the accident, I left the Brooklyn Ghetto and, hours later, landed in the peaceful, college town of Monroe, Louisiana, where a new phase in my life (and my dreaming) was about to begin.

Though God tried many times and ways to make himself known to me, it wasn't until June of 1975 that he was successful. I (accidentally) picked up a copy of Edgar Cayce on ESP, and immediately afterwards read, There is a River, the biography of Edgar Cayce. Not only did those books open the door to spirituality for me, they impressed upon me the importance of dreams. It was when I began writing out my dreams (and a few months later recording them) that I realized the volume of dreaming I was doing. The dreams began giving me advice, laughter, consolation and inspiration, just to name a few of their benefits.

After becoming convinced in the existence of God and Spirit, I decided that I needed to know more about Jesus, so I joined a Southern Baptist Sunday School to learn the New Testament. I had spent my first thirteen years studying Judaism (because I was told I had to by my parents and they were bigger than I was), but, when I began studying Christianity, I wanted to know everything about the Bible from beginning to end. For the next three years, I studied fervently and became grounded in my belief in Spirit.

With this new desire to learn more about God and Spirit, my dreams gave me deeper and deeper insight into spiritual truths. There have been tests along the way (as told in dreams such as "God or Mammon" and "Are You Ready?"). Dreams have also given me choices of spiritual advancement or worldly fame and, so far, with each test, I feel that I have made the correct choice. I hope that I'll continue to make the right choice with each test that follows.

GOD OR MAMMON?

October 1975

A spirit teacher came to me and said, "Do you want to come with me on the spiritual path or do you want to go with them on the path of worldly success and money?" She showed me a room filled with doctors marching up a winding staircase as she spoke. My mind was thinking that worldly success and money were more important, but my heart said, "No, I'll go with you." As soon as I said that, all the cares of the world fell off my shoulders. Then two spirit teachers (a man and a woman) took me into another room. They began pulling out a second skin from my groin region, and it started burning and hurting me. The man said, "Don't worry about it" and continued to pull it out until it completely covered my old body. Suddenly I found myself back home in Brooklyn. I was surprised that no one knew that I had changed, but, on the surface, everything looked the same.

My insight: Although I thought that worldly things were very important, I discovered that I placed spirit foremost in my life, and, because of that, I was transformed.

DON'T WORRY, GOD WILL TAKE CARE OF IT

November 20, 1978

The setting was a doctor's office. Someone wanted x-rays from me. I said, "Don't worry about it." They said that they were worried about it. I said, "Don't worry about it, God will take care of it!" They said, "Oh Yeah? What makes you so certain of that?" "God will take care of it," I said. "Just have confidence and faith and He will take care of everything." There seemed to be some sort of problem of people getting their x-rays back in four days. They were very upset and still had a lot of symptoms. I finally got very indignant and said, "Don't worry; God will do it! He can do anything He wants to do! You just need to have faith!" Finally they had confidence and things were taken care of in four days.

My insight: I was worrying too much and needed to exhibit more faith in God. The answer to my lack of faith was repeated several times so that I would get the message: "Don't worry; God will take care of it."

I Was With Christ

I WAS WITH CHRIST

April 8, 1980

I was with Christ. I held His hands and wept. He said that others needed my prayers and I thought of my parents. When I was holding His hands in mine, He asked me if people were living by the letter of the law or doing the deed? (By this He meant, are people merely going through the motions of the law or are they truly feeling it in their hearts?) I answered, "No. They always do the letter of the law but do not feel it in their hearts."

My insight: We need to feel Christian principals in our hearts and not just mechanically walk through the motions of the physical procedure (like honoring a Holy Day).

GO TELL PETER

September 14, 1980

I was at a Holistic Health Seminar and Olga Worrell said to me, "Go tell Peter that I will pray about when we should return, and, when you receive the direction, then you will know that we need to get together again." It seemed that Peter was a man I knew, and she was telling me to go and tell him that he was Peter (as though he did not understand).

My insight: Olga Worrell is in spirit and at some time in the future she will send me guidance to get together with "Simon Peter".

THE BOOK OF LIFE

February 8, 1981

I had a chart with columns on it, referring to different people. It told the story of your life. Your life was already laid out. I thought it was interesting that my last column showed me taking a high advancement next time, due to what I would achieve in this life.

My insight: My life will be one of spiritual achievement.

SPIRITUAL ORGANIZATION

April 14, 1981

I was at a special convention. There was a young man who was the spiritual leader of this organization or religious group. He was an enlightened being. A group of us were being checked to see if we had any special qualities. When they came to me, they said that I had the beginning stage of Muktananda without having practiced it. This would qualify me for one of the major positions in the spiritual organization. I was going to be in the category that had me in charge of hundreds of thousands. It was related to "Affinity For Plants" — communication with plant life (not growing them). The organization was set up with each box representing one person as follows:

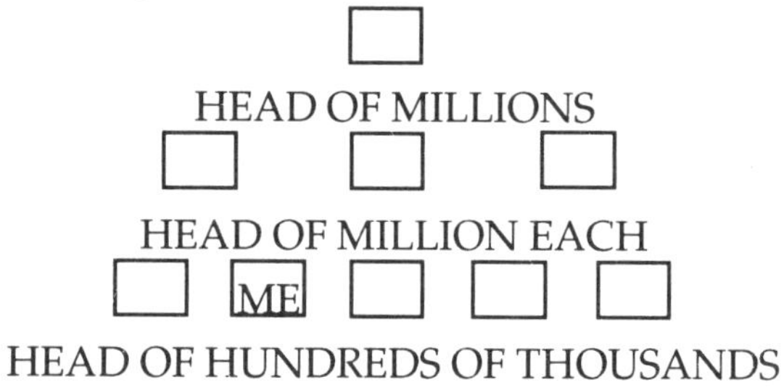

My insight: I was one of the few chosen by Spirit to help the earth in some special way.

HE'LL TELL YOU WHAT TO SAY

December 3, 1982

I was at a class reunion back in tiem. In the banquet room, I approached the organizer's platform. I asked them, "Who will be your main speaker?" They answered, "You are." I was quite surprised and wondered why they hadn't notified me. I then asked them, "What is the topic supposed to be?"
They answered, "Jesus." Again I was surprised and said, "I don't know enough to talk about Jesus." They answered, "Don't worry; He will tell you what to say."

My insight: Spirit will tell me all I need to know.

Dream With Moses

DREAM WITH MOSES

October 11, 1982

At a banquet, I was a waiter placing bread on the tables in large handfuls. I was upset, as the other waiters were not doing their part. Some men (who appeared to be holy men in fancy robes) wanted to speak to Moses. (Moses seemed to be dead with a cloth over his head). All of a sudden, he sat up; he was not dead. But Moses didn't want to speak to the men in fancy robes. Instead he said, "I want Saul." Then I walked up to him and said, "Are you sure you've got the right person? I'm just a lowly waiter." Moses answered, "Yes; you are the one. I want you to assist our Father who will be arriving soon."

My insight: Although I thought of myself as being unworthy, I was willing to serve all; with Moses as its spokesman, Spirit showed me that I was not only worthy, but specifically chosen.

I'M A CHRISTIAN

December 13, 1982

I'm in a banquet hall. It is a religious get together. Representatives are there from many different religions and organizations. I represent the Christian Broadcasting Network.

My insight: I will represent the Christian belief for many.

ARE YOU READY?

September 29, 1984

My girlfriend's mother, Edi, turned to me and asked, "Are you ready to meet Jesus?" I looked her straight in the eye and said, "Not only am I ready, but I'm ready right now."

My insight: Each of us needs to be ready to respond to spirit at all times. This dream made me feel that I am prepared to meet spirit's call whenever it comes.

God Spoke To Me

GOD SPOKE TO ME

December 21, 1982

I thought I was a heathen. All of a sudden I heard a big booming voice say, "I Am That I Am." When I heard the voice, it gave me great strength and faith, enough to build an aqueduct across a mountain top. I looked behind me and saw Joshua behind me on the hill. He appeared to be ill and was going to lean on me to help him walk. Then the voice told me that I'd be led into the desert to learn more about Jesus and that only prophets and children of Cana could go. "But I am an unworthy heathen," I said, "so I guess that leaves me out." "No," answered the voice. "That leaves you in. You are a child of Cana."

My insight: Once again, I thought of myself as being unworthy. But God spoke to me and gave me the confidence and strength I needed to follow the spiritual path. Jesus was the answer.

OLD AND THE NEW

March 29, 1984

I am wearing my star of David with the cross. I was asked what it was. I said, "Jesus was born a Jew. It is what I am. I am the old and the new."

My insight: I was born a Jew but consider myself a Christian-Jew in belief.

GOD HAS ENTERED

I was looking for my star of David in different places but couldn't find it. Finally a voice says, "The man has now departed, and God has entered.'

My insight: I used to wear the star of David with the cross but had forgotten and left it at home when I took a trip to Holland. I took this to mean that I had gone beyond symbols, and that now God was firmly in my heart, mind and soul-not just an ornament that I wore.

ROOM WHERE STAR OF DAVID IS KEPT

February 2, 1990

I am in a motel and oversleep. As I start to gather my belongings, I notice my star of David with the cross in it and also a cross of mine. I said, "So that is where I left it." At this particular motel, if something is left, nobody touches it until the owner reclaims it. I felt good knowing that it was there waiting for me.

My insight: I had lost my star of David with the cross, but this dream made me see the concept of, "If it's yours, you can't lose it, and if it isn't yours, you can't hold on to it."

POWER OF THE HOLY SPIRIT

December 11, 1984

A woman's child was crying. I said, "Maybe I could give him a muscle adjustment to help." She said something like, "What?" or "How?" I said, "I am Dr. Shaye." She said, "Oh, you know Dr. Shaye?" I said, "No; I am Dr. Shaye." Again she said, "Oh, you know him?" I finally shouted, "I am Dr. Shaye." Then she said, "Do you have any experience?" "I was told "you shall have the keys to the kingdom," I said. "Anything else?" She asked. "Yes," I said. "I was told that I would do this by the power of the Holy Spirit."

My insight: I will be empowered by Spirit to help many people.

Who Will Qualify?

WHO WILL QUALIFY?

February 17, 1988

I'm in a room with a large number of people. They are waiting to see who will qualify to go to Christ (or Jesus). I thought to myself, "It won't be me because I didn't do anything to earn the right to go." A number of the people thought that they were ready. Then some people came into the room and took two or three women and then they took me. I was quite shocked and could barely stand, but they were prepared for that, laughingly telling me that they knew I would be uneasy on my feet. I was ecstatic knowing that I was being chosen and was leaving right away. We walked past my wallet on the floor and I thought I needed to pick it up, but then I thought to myself, "No; it doesn't matter. Neither money nor anything else matters; At that moment I felt a great sense of release, like a child at the end of school. I knew I was going to heaven. The man and the woman seemed angelic, like they were there to take me home. I would no longer need to think about anything anymore, as though everything was taken care of for me.

My insight: The theme of unworthiness repeats itself once again. I am shown that I am worthy and that, if I continue in the direction I am going, everything will be taken care of.

ORDER FROM ABOVE

December 29, 1984

I am a pilot. Orders from up above are to fly my plane upside down. The other co-pilots are against it. The higher-ups want to see if I will carry out an order no matter how dangerous it sounds. I feel that I will go ahead.

My insight: I will do whatever Spirit asks of me.

WE ARE ALL ONE FAMILY

October 28, 1990

I'm talking to some people about the spiritual hierarchy in heaven. I tell them I'm a messenger (an envoy). I put my hand right through some table. I tell these people about a special kind of propulsion and also about the people in control of gasoline engines who didn't want to let go of their control. I said that we could have done it a long time ago. Then they asked me, "Which is the correct spiritual reality?" I tell them that it's all the same, Jew or Moslem, it doesn't matter. I said, "The thing that sums it all up is that we are all one." "One What?" They asked. I answered, "One Family, that's it."

My insight: We are all God's children. If we would acknowledge that fact, we would realize that we are all brothers and sisters, and, therefore, one family.

CHRIST COMING AGAIN SOON

September 24, 1992

There were poor people in a Latin American country setting. Fliers were being distributed about Christ coming again soon. A poor woman who received the flier was tortured to make her retract her statement. In a dungeon, you could see her broken, cut body. In another room, a slave looked up toward a fenced-in window. I was peeking in the window. I seemed to be that which was foretold would come. As the slave looked up at me, the gate to the window suddenly unlocked, and he realized that he was to be set free of all his chains. I was the messenger, but then I became the slave who was set free. (I was more than one person in the dream).

My insight: When we look to Christ, all earthly chains are undone. This dream gives tremendous hope to the oppressed, with its message of a miracle on the horizon.

I AM BATMAN

I was covered with an after-birth-like film. Someone had bumped into something that appeared to be a baby crib. I pulled the skin-like film off of me (like a skin or blanket), and, when I finally completed the process, I was Batman (uniform and all). Then someone said, "Let's test him with a simple dream first."

My insight: When I am born again in spirit, I will become a new person, endowed with special abilities. I will be tested by way of dreams, as to when I am ready.

GOD OR A MILLION DOLLARS - GOD IS MY CHOICE

I was having a conversation with someone about witnessing to kids, without them realizing it. I said, "Any time you talk about spirit to anybody, you are witnessing. In that sense, it is easy for me to witness because if I were offered the choice between direct communion with God right now or a million dollars, there would be no choice. There isn't enough money or sex to tempt me as compared to desiring God communciation, When you tell that to people, you are witnessing."

My insight: Spirit is the most important thing in my life, and, by stating that openly, one is witnessing.

Chapter Two

HEALING DREAMS

INTRODUCTION TO HEALING DREAMS

In 1973, I attended a workshop on non-physical (intuitive) diagnosis, with the intention of disproving the concept. At the time, I had no belief in Spirit, which included anything psychic (or of the soul.)

The class was shown how to communicate with the body by asking it questions. Answers were received through a sensation felt in the hands. There were twenty students who attended the workshop. They went to learn it; I went to attack it. Months later, to my dismay, I discovered I could sense responses, like the instructor taught in the course, with my hands.

This strange gift made me uneasy at the time, since I was an Atheist. I had no idea what to do with this ability or how it fit into my life. It wasn't logical and didn't go along with my way of thinking.

This ability finally led me to pick up a book on ESP, hoping it would give me an answer to what I was doing. It did. In fact, it turned into my Damascus Road. My belief in God was born at that moment!

My rebirth unleashed a desire to be of service to God. Because of that desire, I was ultimately led to the realization that God had bestowed upon me the gift of healing. This gift has been explained to me in the dreams that follow. When I found that I could do healing based upon the symbols in my dreams, I began placing more significance in what my dreams were saying in terms of what will be and who I am (Visionary Dreams).

REARRANGE ENERGY FIELDS

September 22, 1981

I am telling people about my treatment. I can treat them physically, which most people prefer, or psychically. I can rearrange the energy fields just by stepping into the room and waving my hands over the energy fields.

My insight: Healing begins the instant one is in close proximity to another who is receptive to the healing.

Sign Of The Cross

"THE GATE WAS LOCKED....."
BLOCKING MY PATH!

"WITH THE SIGN OF THE CROSS.....
THE LOCK OPENS & FALLS AWAY!"

SIGN OF THE CROSS

November 8, 1981

It seems as though I am in a church building and help Spirit manifest somehow. I am doing various psychic things. Leaving this church through a door or gate that has a lock on it, I say to the lock, "Okay, Lock," and make the sign of the cross at it. The lock then opens and the door swings open. Some people say, "Look; we have Christ in our midst." I say, "No; There he is." Somehow I help (Him) manifest visibility. One of them said to me, "Wow; you're just great." I said, "No; I'm not anything. Maybe I am here just to help Him manifest the Christ." The people say, "That sounds reasonable."

My insight: I found that I could heal with the sign of the cross. By my own ability, I would not be able to do healing, but, by the power of God working through me, all things would be possible.

CAN TREAT ANYTHING

October 1, 1981

I am talking to someone about how I can treat anything with energy. I said that it was instanteous through any object, even a diamond, and over any distance. The man that I was talking to told me that he would have to be sure and drew out a pistol and shot me in the chest. I waved my hand over the are, and it seemed as though the bullet fell to the ground. I wasn't certain whether it was real or just a blank since I had waved it off and wasn't hurt I was extrememly angry at this guy who needed proof to the extent that he would threaten my life, though. I walked out saying that he had lost his chance and that I wouldn't work for him.

My insight: Though the healing energy has the potential to correct anything, there will be some disbelievers along the way. They will pose no problem to me, but I should shake the dust from my feet and move on to those I can serve.

WHO I AM

December 17, 1981

On a street, two guys challenge me to a gun duel. I am in a quandary. There are two of them, and they have guns. I am trying to figure out the solution on my own, but there is no way I can do this. I say, "The time has come. I have to come forth and say who I am. I am the Christ. It is time for me to announce this." I thought of the Jewish people who wouldn't understand. "Who else can I get as a second," I thought. "I don't know who else I can place in this situation, so I have to state who I am. That is the answer." I still felt nervous about the solution. I wouldn't have understanding from a lot of people by coming out with this at this time.

My insight: We are the body of Christ. When we come forth and claim our true identity, conflict ends. (I found that I could also heal with the "I Am" symbol.) For me, the "I Am" symbol stands for God the Father, in the trinity (Father, Son and Holy Spirit) all three are healing.

CHANGE ENERGY IN ELECTROMAGNETIC FIELDS

March 7, 1982

I told a husband and wife that I could treat the woman by working with her electromagnetic fields. I said that I was restricted on what I could do in my practice (clinic) at home, but not when I travel. The husband was doubtful. I said, "I can change the energy in the electromagnetic fields which in turn will change and correct the physical. You don't have to believe; just see what happens." The man said that sounded logical to see what response we got. Then all three of us went into the back room to treat her.

My insight: My intuitive mind had to convince my logical mind that the energy could work.

HEALING BY NAME ONLY

April 14, 1982

There is a prayer list of people's names. I asked if I could help people without knowing who they were but knew their name.

My insight: Whether I know a person or not is irrelevant. Spirit knows one's intent and will complete the healing process.

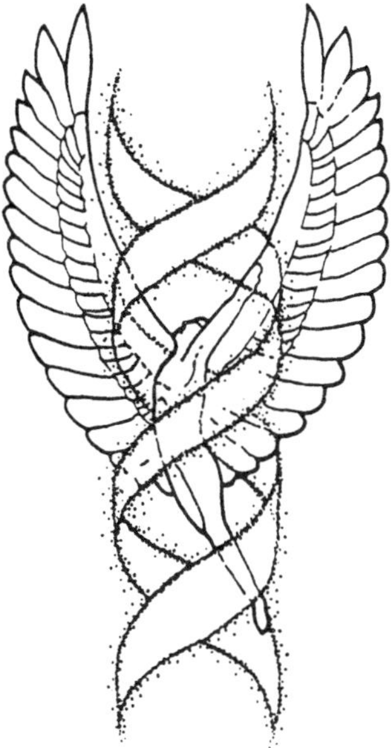

HEALING BY THE WORD

February 26, 1983

People were hurt and needed help. I said to them, "I just need to say "The Word" and you will be okay."

My insight: I found that I could heal by just saying "The Word". ["In the beginning was the word, and the word was with God, and the word was God." John 1:1]

IN THE NAME OF JESUS

September 1, 1992

I am in a room with older people. An old woman is giving out candy (Red Hots Candy) that she says is healing. I play along with her and put my hand on her shoulder and send healing energy into that area; then I move it around to different parts of her arm and upper chest clavicle area. People in the room notice what I do for her and, after I sit back down, they gather around me, even though someone is speaking up front. They extend their arms to me asking if I can help this or that. I help each one that asks. Up front, a speaker has a large black man to come in that has an unusual illness. His stomach is distended and looks like a small boy. He has discussions with the boy configuration. The man speaking says, "This man is a grave digger and has a rare bone disease." I suddenly feel strange all over and start walking toward the speaker and the man. I feel filled with the Spirit with tremendous power surging through me. The winds increase all around me and the black man is now in a small cage. In a powerful voice, I say, "In the name of Jesus the Christ, come out of there." At first I am not aware of any change, but the person seems to be healed, as the spirit possessing him departs. Gradually the energy and wind decrease and I slowly make my way back to my seat. People are shocked at what they experienced. I feel subdued and grateful for what has transpired with me playing a part. As I take my seat, the people around me are whispering among themselves. Someone asks, "How did you know what that was?" I said, "Something wasn't right. He was too familiar with and wanted to get rid of an obvious awkward problem." A feeling comes over me and Spirit takes over. An important speaker comes up to me and asks if I could stay and meet some person. I say, "I can't wait, as I have to meet someone in New Jersey, but you can come with me." I put my hands in front of me and start flying like a car toward the area I am going.

My insight: Healing work will progress from working on physical ailments to removing negative spiritual influences, with spirit guiding me as to when and how.

WE KNOW WHO YOU ARE

September 7, 1992

I am walking behind some couple amidst the rubble of city streets (a lot of objects as well as buildings). Finally, I sit down behind the couple. A nurse puts some x-rays of their child (Boy?) up on a screen and tells her some technical words that sound like "locked knee." The x-rays seemed to show the knee cap at a strange location. I wanted desperately to help, but I knew I couldn't say anything. I wanted to ask, "Do you want to be rid of that or something similar?" Instead, I raised my hand in front of me trying not to be too conspicuous and made the sign of the cross at the x-rays. Then I got up and left. I was carrying some packages. One of them seemed like a huge loaf of bread. Before I could get out the door, I heard footsteps. The couple had hurried after me. One of them said to me, "We know who you are." I answered, "You do?" They said, "Yes; you must be a healer." The nurse said that a miracle occurred after you did something at the x-ray and wondered if you would do it for the others also. "If I knew she thought that, I would have. You are right; I am a famous healer who travels the world trying to help people. My basic occupation is that of a chiropractor, but I do "healing" also. I left there saying, "We will see you at the North Pole." (It seemed like I was making a reference to Santa Claus).

My insight: My desire to help and heal will be more and more well received in the future.

SIGN OF THE CROSS PURIFIES LAND

September 20, 1992

I was walking around people telling them that I could dowse with my hands, as Christopher Bird (the author of the Secret World of Plants) had said. I could use my hands to sense energy, then make the sign of the cross at it and change the energy. We were doing this in a field with a group of seven to ten people. Someone would say that they sensed something in a certain place, then I would make the sign of the cross at it, and they would say it was changed. We would go around the field doing this experiment and propose theories, wondering what we could do with it. The large open field was definitely changed. Even for people who thought there would be no change, there was no doubt about it. Then, afterwards, we had the thought that maybe we could try this with T.V. by speaking to the T.V. set asking, "Would you like to experiment on doing some good work?' If the answer was "Yes," we'd zap it (or maybe zap different shows).

My insight: The Christ energy can be used to correct any lack, illness or even negative energy.

Chapter Three

EASY TO APPLY DREAMS

INTRODUCTION

I have grouped the following dreams in a chapter by themselves, as they express ideas that I understand and can do something about in a very direct manner. Very few of my more than 15,000 dreams say or direct me as simply as these do. For this reason, I believe they deserve special recognition.

A NEW PATH

In January of 1976, I went to Phoenix, Arizona, to attend an A.R.E Holistic Health Seminar. I arrived late at night, checked in at the Safari Hotel, went to sleep and dreamt the following:

I was walking down a street when a camel came along. I got up on the camel's back, and it took me to a railroad track. The tracks were bright stainless steel. The camel proceeded to take me down the tracks to a part of town that I had never been to before.

My insight: When I awoke from this dream, I thought, "What a silly dream." Early that next morning, I decided to go for a walk. I walked about a block until I came to a street corner and looked up at the sign. The name of the street was (Camelback Road). Camelback Road would take me to a place that I'd never been (The A.R.E. and Holistic Health Seminar). I was about to be introduced to ideas I'd never before encountered.

I had a question: *Is chiropractic the correct profession for me?*

I had a dream:

There were a lot of upheavals, with buildings and equipment destroyed. I was talking to a group of people and said, "With all this destruction, I am so glad that I am a Chiropractor, as I don't need any special equipment. All I need is my hands. I am the perfect doctor.'

My insight: I took this dream as a positive statement that I was on the correct path. Chiropractic was the perfect choice for me.

I had a question: *Where should I live?*

I had a dream:

I was a little baby in a crib (very tiny, about one inch long) and was unable to move. Beside me was a bigger baby in a bigger crib, running around and was very mobile. Although the bigger baby could move all around, as hard as I tried, I could not. In this dream a large plant was beside the baby bed. It was revolving. Finally, it stopped and pointed one long leaf at me and said. "The other baby can move because it is bigger. You, too, can move when you are bigger."

My insight: At that time in my life, one of the major concerns facing me was whether or not to come back to Monroe to practice. I thought that I should go away to a bigger city. When I considered that dream and what it could mean, I realized that it was saying that I was not yet ready for the big city and that Monroe was where I should begin. I'm to stay where I am until I have grown (matured) and then I can move if I desire.

SHOULD I WRITE?

I had a question: *Should I write anything?*

This was the dream that followed.

I was in a gunfight in the Old West. My opponent reached for his pistols in his holsters. I reached for my holsters and drew out two pencils and shot him with them.

I decided to write.

BROTHER NEEDS MORE EDUCATION

1976

In this dream, I was told to tell my brother, Nat, that without further education, he was incomplete.

My insight: I told my older brother, Nat, this dream when he was working at Yale University. He said that he used my dream as the push he was looking for to leave Yale. He felt that he had received a higher calling, and went back to school for four more years and became a chiropractor.

I WAS TOXIC

Dream:
I was a drug smuggler. I was stopped by the police, and I thought, "I hope they don't check my trunk, as I have old drugs stored in my spare tire."

My insight: The trunk was the body and the spare tire was symbolic of body fat (spare tire around one's middle) and old drugs (old chemicals) that were in my body from the past. I took this to mean that I was toxic and needed to purify my body. I chose occasional fasting to help purify my body of old chemicals.

I WAS ROBIN HOOD

I was Robin Hood. As in the original tale, I met Little John, crossing a stream on a log bridge. We started fighting with long staffs. Unlike the original, we fought with metal staffs. Finally, he was able to get his staff around my throat and said to me, "Do you give?" When I didn't answer, he asked again, "Do you give?" I finally answered, "I give, I give; you don't have to be so rough."

My insight: I wondered why we were fighting with metal staffs rather than wooden ones, then realized that the metal staff reminded me of a barbell. Weight lifting was choking me. At the time of this dream, I was working out with weight lifting six to seven days per week. The dream was telling me I needed to give in and train less. I did just that and cut back to three days per week.

DON'T TAKE THE 9:15 TRAIN

My last night at Findhorn in June 1982, I had the following dream:

I was heading for the train station to catch the 9:15 train. First, I came to a stop sign and couldn't go any further. Next, I turned down a street going the wrong way. It seemed that no matter which street I took, it was wrong. Finally, a voice spoke to me and said, "You'll never make the 9:15.

My insight: When I awoke from this dream, I was scheduled to leave on the 9:15 train for home, but, because of the dream, I decided I wasn't supposed to take that train, and stayed later. At 9:30, a friend called and gave me some very important information (which is a story all of its own). This same man has appeared in numerous dreams since as a teacher. Had I not listened to my dream and taken the 9:15 anyway, a piece to the puzzle of my life may have never been answered.

Chapter Four

CAYCE DREAMS

INTRODUCTION

The dreams in this chapter are dedicated to Edgar Cayce and the A.R.E. (Association for Research and Enlightenment).

My initial interest in spirituality was kindled by reading books about the life of Edgar Cayce, such as Edgar Cayce on E S P, Edgar Cayce's Story Of Jesus, etc. It was due to the Cayce material that I changed from an Atheist to a believing, non-denominational, Christian Jew, who fervently wanted to serve spirit as his ultimate goal in life. For that reason, I feel a strong connection to my Cayce and A.R.E. dreams.

Edgar Cayce's life, also, served as an ideal for me. I found him to be a very giving and modest man, who was firmly grounded in his Christian beliefs. He lived by those Christian principles his entire life, and without knowing it, passed them on to many others. I am certain that the spirit of Cayce is aware of the impact he had, and continues to have on my life, and occasionally visits me in a dream, reminding me of our connection. That is why, when he is mentioned or appears in a dream, I feel a sense of gratitude and consider it as a sign of importance.

MAKE ROOM FOR ME

May 22, 1978

I am at a Holistic Health Conference and decide to put castor oil packs on my hands and lie down, but the man sitting next to me is too close. I say, "Excuse me; would you make room for me?" The man was Hugh Lynn Cayce.

My insight: I am asking the A.R.E. (symbolized by Hugh Lynn Cayce) to make room for me. The special healing abilities of my hands (symbolized by castor oil packs on them) will be the item of interest.

HOW I BECAME A CHRISTIAN

February 10, 1981

I was traveling and people were asking me questions. One man asked, "What are you doing?" I said, "I am lecturing to different groups and professions on Holistic Health which includes diet, manipulation, exercise, detoxification, mental attitude and spiritual awareness (including prayer, meditation and dream study)." The people said, "Wow; that sounds marvelous." Then some man said, "Tell me how you became a Christian." (I was wearing my star of David with the cross in it.) I said, "That's a long story, but it all began with Edgar Cayce in 1975."

My insight: I owe a lot of my present beliefs to a book I read in 1975, "There Is A River," the biography of Edgar Cayce, which opened the door to Spirit for me.

THE SABBATICAL BICYCLE

October 14, 1982, 4:26 a.m.

A spiritual teacher gives me some special bread. He then says, "Do you know what a sabbatical bicycle is?" I answer, "No; I don't."

[When I awoke from that dream, I liked the concept of a sabbatical or a spiritual leave of absence. Before I went back to sleep, I said, "I surely wish that God would tell me what the bicycle stands for." An hour and a half later, I awoke with the following dream:]

I'M RENTING EDGAR CAYCE'S HOUSE

October 14, 1982, 6:00 a.m.

I am renting a large house. It is almost paid for. My Father is the landlord. It used to be Edgar Cayce's house. In the basement is this beautiful bicycle without its front wheel. Hugh Lynn Cayce is telling me about the bicycle.

My insight: I am almost in full (house almost paid for) possession of certain spiritual (Father is landlord or used to be Edgar Cayce's) gifts. The direction is still uncertain (missing front wheel).

EDGAR CAYCE

February 14, 1986

I wrote an article which was written up in a journal. A group was asking me questions. They asked me what my religious beliefs were. I said that I was basically a Christian, but thought that God had expressed himself through numerous famous souls, like Jesus, Buddha, Mohammed and Moses; as well as within individuals who would take the time to listen. As I was saying that, Edgar Cayce was sitting there and said, "Absolutely right." With any particular question, you could ask yourself, "How would Edgar Cayce have answered?" After awhile you knew how Edgar Cayce would have answered. I felt that I had graduated from the course.

My insight: Edgar Cayce was very instrumental in my going from an Atheist to a non-denominational Christian Jew. Because of him, I became firmly convinced of Spirit. To me, his life was a model of Christian living and a good example to follow.

Chapter Five

VISIONARY DREAMS

PART I

(Sequential)

INTRODUCTION

The following dreams deal with an ongoing, common theme. They are what I call my "football dreams" about "Team Phoenix". I am rather partial to these dreams for several reasons, the first one being my fondness for football; secondly, the majority of the dreams have me playing quarterback (my favorite position); and third and most importantly, the message that I will be guided and assisted to provide a great service to mankind.

In the dreams, there is a football game being played (which represents life). There are old pros (enlightened souls or souls with very special abilities or gifts of the spirit), coming into this dimension to help mankind at this important time in history, a time that has been predicted by Edgar Cayce, Ruth Montgomery and, most importantly, the Bible, to be a time of such momentous events as earth changes, Armageddon and the second coming. Their predictions indicate that the world will be subjected to some major changes toward the end of this century, as the earth shifts on its axis causing unbelievable hardships (the likes of which we've never known before). When this stage unfolds, I am certain that I will be called upon to help mankind in a special way (as is foretold by this series of dreams). Most of these dreams place me in the position of quarterback (or leadership). I feel it a great privilege that spirit has entrusted me with this important part to aid my fellow man.

This story unfolds with the dreams as follows: special souls are coming to earth to assist with the many changes that will occur shortly; I will be a leader (quarterback) amidst these special souls (old pros); I will be given special abilities (gifts of the Spirit) to help our side win (best offensive player, special ability, etc.). We will aid and guide (before and during the changes) and rebuild from the ashes afterwards. By definition, the Phoenix symbol is a legendary bird, held to live for centuries, and then to burn itself to death and rise fresh and young from its ashes. "Team Phoenix" will have this special role to play. Some of the souls are from other solar systems (spaceship with football players). We will aid in fighting the war between the sons of light and the sons of darkness (the opposing team-symbolic of certain corrupt aspects of government and big business). I will remain a chiropractor for as long as I can, but, when the time is right, I will step forth in power (symbolized by Samson Dream — "Are you he who used to be Samson?") I will enter the conflict at its end (last two minutes) when spirit tells me it's time (the sponsor will bring me in).

I am thankful to be given this position of service, and I pray that, when the time comes, I will do all that is asked of me. We will all have an important part to play (there are no small parts). So please listen to your dreams; you might find yourself playing football with me on "Team Phoenix."

TEAM WITH OLD PROS
I

April 12, 1980

There was an athletic event going on. More and more of the players were being used (as expressed by stacks of many jerseys) until they reached the jerseys of some of the old pros. As the regular players were finished, more and more of these old pros were taking their place. I was on an escalator going up. The guy next to me said that I was going to be the quarterback and these all-pros were in the backfield with me. Still, I felt very confident. The guy asked me what my grades were. I told him that I had better than a "B" average, as I didn't want to seem to brag, but my average was actually closer to an "A" average.

My insight: The game of life. More and more of the enlightened souls were being brought back, and I am going to be a leader amongst them, for this special time in history (second coming, earth changes, Armageddon, etc.).

TEAM WITH OLD PROS
II

May 2, 1981

There was a football game being played, but it appeared to be a movie. Someone said that it was unusual for them to change quarterbacks once the game was underway, but the sponsor of the game brought me in. I go out on the field to the huddle and am looking at the different professional football players (retired) [old pros] playing the various positions. Then the coach says to me, "So you're Young." I answer, "Yeah," realizing he's saying my name for the cameras. He seems disappointed that I'm just standing there, and I realize that they brought me in to get the team going. I take off my jacket (my key ring was on my belt with the Phoenix name) and I begin giving them a talk about winning. I tell them. "If you want to win, you've got to stop your opponent and then, by your effort, you have to score. They get all fired up, which is what the coach wanted (my dynamic personality getting the team moving). We break the huddle and do a drop pass to a man behind the lines, who in turn passes it to another man for a touchdown. I say, "That looked a little phony the way he caught the ball with the opposing players letting him. Next we score again, but this time with a beautiful pass with the receiver wide open for the touchdown. The other team then scores, but we are ahead by a touchdown.

My insight: The team of enlightened souls are already here. At the right time, God (The Sponsor) will bring me in to lead them. The Phoenix symbol may be the rebuilding or Armageddon and them rebuilding. The name "Young" may mean that I may still be fairly young when this takes place.

OLD PROS QUARTERBACK

October 7, 1981

I'm talking to two guys. They are quarterbacks. I say, "If they don't do a good job, they will bring me out of retirement (it seemed that I was a retired quarterback [old pro?]). Then I pick up a football and throw it to someone across this pool area. It bounces off the wall. My arm was really out of shape. I thought I would take the ball and go practice to get my arm back in shape.

My insight: I'm getting ready to get back in the game. I was an old pro (one of the enlightened souls) coming back to lead. I was getting ready by warming up.

BEST OFFENSIVE PLAYER

July 18, 1983

Football Game: I'm the best offensive player, the quarterback.

My insight: I will be a leader who, with very special abilities, will help our side do what needs to be done.

OUTER SPACE FOOTBALL TEAM

December 22, 1981

Outer Space Dream. I was in a spacecraft with a football team.

My insight: A number of these souls with special abilities are from another solar system. There are many dreams (like this one) where I experienced the thought rather than saw it acted out. It wasn't like watching a movie unwind. When the dream is more of a feeling experience, it is very difficult to describe with words.

Outerspace Football Team

ONE OF THE GREAT PLAYERS

October 31, 1984

I was put into the game. The players didn't know who I was, but the coach and I knew something they didn't. Out on the field, I didn't have on my red jersey so that they would know that I was on their side. I am an old quarterback. The announcer recognizes me and says, "Now we are going to see one of the truly great players."

My insight: The other enlightened souls on" Team Phoenix" don't recognize me. The coach and announcer (guides) know about my spiritual gifts, which are considerable.

SUPER PLAYER

November 8, 1984

I was some type of super player in a football game. I could play any position. I asked the coach to send me in so that the team could win. He said, "Okay; call your own number and play where you want."

My insight: I have great abilities. I asked spirit to let me help and was given the okay.

SPECIAL ABILITY

January 15, 1985

I was at football practice; the coaches wanted my speed on the team.

My insight: I have unique abilities which could help our side do what needs to be done.

Used to Be Samson

USED TO BE SAMSON

December 5, 1985

There is a football game being played. The field is a rock solid foundation of a large church that was torn down. I caught the ball and went for a touchdown. A little old man cleaning a sword says, "Aren't you he who used to be called Samson?" I answer, "Yes." He says, "Use your present identity as long as you can and when you have to use the name of Samson, use it in honor.

My insight: "Team Phoenix's" playing field is the original Christian principle (rock solid foundation). The battle between the forces of light and the forces of darkness will be waged on this field with me being empowered (when you have to use the name of Samson) by Spirit. Once I'm entrusted with these special abilities, I am to use them with honor and justice.

LAST TWO MINUTES

January 23, 1986

I was talking to a pro quarterback. I was going into the game right at the last two minutes as quarterback.

My insight: The game of life is already set in motion. I will be brought into the battle right at the end (Armageddon, Second Coming, etc.).

SHARI WAS A QUARTERBACK

August 21, 1986

There was a football game being played. An unfamiliar player was called into the game. When the player came into the huddle, the person took off her helmet, at which time a full head of long blond hair fell out. My girlfriend, Shari, was the unfamiliar player. I said, "Shari, I didn't know you played football." She was going to be a quarterback on this football team. I was going to try her out with contact, as she hadn't played with contact yet.

My insight: Shari has an unrecognized ability to help in this spiritual warfare. (Trying her our with contact probably meant that she must be tested to see if she has the courage to carry out her part).

SPACESHIP LANDS

September 10, 1986

There was a football game being played. A spaceship lands with sounds and words. The words are saying something to the effect of "All good things, use them in peace." Fear turned to a strong sense of inner peace and joy.

My insight: Beings from outer space, guides and angels are motivating, encouraging and helping us to carry out our mission. Their message is one of good will.

MANY FOOTBALL GAMES

March 24, 1987

There were a number of football games being played. The players were in prayer until game time. I realized there were many teams, and I play many positions.

My insight: There are many enlightened souls here to help in this confrontation, waiting in prayer, until the time is right. I'm to help in many different ways.

MY TEAM WILL WIN

December 22, 1987

Football game: Opponents were the Washington Redskins. In the opposing team's locker room were certain corrupt business people. I wished them luck, but I knew without a doubt my team would win. In the game, I thought I would get the ball.

My insight: Our main spiritual opponents will be certain corrupt representatives of Washington (or government and big business), but I know my team (Spirit) will win.

FOOTNOTE:

As I mentioned in the introduction to Visionary Dreams (PartI), certain souls will be coming into this dimension to help mankind at this important time in history. One of the problems these souls will have to deal with relates to the following passage from the book of Revelation: "And he causeth all, both small and great, rich and poor, free and bond, to receive a mark in their right hand, or in their foreheads, and that no man might buy or sell, save he that had the mark, or the name of the beast, or the number of his name. Here is wisdom. Let him that hath understanding count the number of the beast: for it is the number of a man; and his number is six hundred three score and six." Revelation 13:16-18

"If any man worship the beast and his image, and receive his mark in his forehead, or in his hand, the same shall drink of the wine of the wrath of God, which is poured out without mixture into the cup of his indignation; and he shall be tormented with fire and brimstone in the presence of the holy angels, and in the presence of the lamb. And the smoke of their torment ascendeth up for ever and ever; and they have no rest day or night, who worship the beast and his image, and whosoever receiveth the mark of his name." Revelation 14:9-10,11

It is my belief that this passage from Revelation relates to the very near future and has to do with the money system, a cashless society and the bar codes listed on credit cards, etc., (or computer marks). This will be a great evil confronting mankind and the only answer (how to buy and sell without the mark) will come from Spirit. I believe that certain souls will be directed as to how to deal with this in an appropriate way and will help and guide others, based upon what will be shown to them.

PERSEVERANCE

October 29, 1991

I win an award for best quarterback. Giving advice to other players about staying with it, I say, "The first year was awkward; the second year, better; this year we went all the way to victory. So stay at it because you never know what can happen."

My insight: Don't give up the battle of good versus evil. In the long run, perseverance will win out. As a leader, I will make certain we stay with the fight until victory is achieved.

GOD'S WHITE HORSE

August 30, 1991

There was a football game. I wasn't certain I'd be able to play on the team. I wanted to play in the game and do what I have to do, as I love the game. I went into a building where there were three trophies. The first place trophy is beautiful. It has three tiers with figures on it and some religious symbols. I said, " The first place trophy is great and I am going to use that as a motivational factor, if I can first get into the game and have a chance to play." I went to a place where many people were waiting for me. I was hoping to get into the game, but it seemed as though they wanted me to ride this big white horse at the head of the procession like the king. I got on the horse, and stood the horse up on two legs and put my hand up (like the Lone Ranger). It looked great to have this marching troop beside me, with me standing up on the horse. I stood up on the horse a couple of times and finally came down very gracefully.

As I gently came down, I handed the reigns to someone. Then I threw a banner up as I greeted the crowd. There was an old man, and I realized the horse was his. I said to him, "Thank you for this opportunity to do this." I felt honored by the part I had been given.

My insight: God will give me his horse to enter the football game. Although I didn't know if I qualified, God chose me for a place of honor.

God's White Horse

WHO IS ON OUR SIDE?

April 19, 1992

Football game: we were deciding who was going to be on our side. They kicked off without waiting for me. I ran in and caught the ball on a bounce and made a perfect run for a touchdown.

My insight: People may not know who to believe or who is telling the truth; spirit will ultimately have to decide who is on the side of righteousness. The battle will start before I get involved, but, when I do, I will help my side on to victory.

USE YOUR ASSISTANT PLAYERS

September 14, 1992

I seemed to be watching a football game on T.V. It was a very tight game (like the Super Bowl). The New England Patriots were playing the Cleveland Browns, with the score, 25 to 23. There was a delay, so the quarterback had to waste a time out. They needed a first down, but the quarterback called a play where he'd run with the ball behind the line of scrimmage. It was a quarterback scramble, but the defense hit all the spots and tackled him in the backfield. New England lost the game, as they didn't get a first down. It seemed very stupid that Steve Grogin (the quarterback) did a quarterback sweep, as he was very old. There were players in the backfield who were much faster than he was, and he should have used them.

My insight: I should rely more on my helpers (angels and Spirit guides) who are better equipped to handle certain problems than I am. Consciously, I'm just a body, but by relying on Spirit, I have all the power of heaven behind me.

MY FRONT LINE IS THE SAINTS

1994

I was in a football game as the quarterback. I broke the huddle and went up to my front line. They were these huge angels with wings.

My insight: I am protected by Angels. Whatever my mission is, it will be carried out as I have powerful beings to assist and protect me.

I BECAME THE COACH

1994

I was told that I wouldn't play in the game even though I was one of the most outstanding performers. I was too important, so I was being moved to become the coach as I knew best how to use all the players for the highest good.

My insight: Spirit was moving me up to a higher position. Though I was disappointed, I knew God knew best how to use people for the highest good.

Chapter Five

VISIONARY DREAMS

PART II

(Non-Sequential)

INTRODUCTION

I have grouped the following dreams as visionary and non-sequential, but they also seem to have a common theme. Over and over, I have dreams that state that this is not my true home; that I am here on a special mission; that I have been given special abilities (gifts of the Spirit); and that there is a tremendous amount of help being provided to me from Spirit.

EXAMPLES

Not My True Home
(I'm from another planet; another world)

Special Mission
(Mission from the commander; special training by Spirit; important role in psychic warfare;

help confront evil for many; show the way; Spirit transforming me; etc.)

Special Abilities
(Super powers within; special, honor class; keys to kingdom)

Help From Spirit
(Training by Spirit; Spirit guides working on me; divinely protected; Spirit knows me and will help; direct reporting to commander; I have large powerful angels with me; mission from God; angels will come and get me; Spirit going to transform me to carry out mission).

SUPER POWER WITHIN

May 26, 1979

I have super powers, but have to hide them. The powers are within. I didn't come to use them for just anything. There is some greater purpose.

My insight: I have abilities within that cannot be made known until a higher purpose unfolds.

SPECIAL SCHOOL WITH ONE HONOR CLASS

May 1, 1980

I am talking about a special school. I hear the comment being made, "In this school there is only one honor class in the entire school." At the first row section, the teacher says, "There is only one honor student in 1500 students, and we all know who that one student is." The teacher points to me. I say, "I don't know how I am supposed to learn by myself." He answer, "You just had a good lesson. You had a half hour with one teacher and whole hour with another." I was thinking of prayer; I was talking about some type of Math and Universal Law. I was this very bright person and had written a good story and was telling my folks about it. Everything had been written except the last paragraph which was in my mind. With tears in my eyes, I realized I had received the answer. I then went back to my room, knowing everything would be taken care of.

My insight: I know more than I realize. I am a soul with very special gifts and abilities.

THREE POWERS

October 1, 1980

This was a long dream with disaster. A building collapsed. I was a special person (Group Captain) with three powers:

1. I was strong enough to take care of anyone (who endangered me).

2. I could survive without food (had some special energy supply).

3. I could travel back in time (could prevent a catastrophe from occurring).

My insight: I have gifts of the Spirit that I'm not aware of.

BANKS FLOODED

December 14, 1980

I was Superman. A bank building was flooded. I lifted the entire building to let the water drain out of it. Then I dove head first into the ground by a fire hydrant to correct it.

My insight: The money system will develop serious problems. This has been prophesied (See Revelation 13: 16-18 & Rev. 14: 9-11) . . . it will be difficult to buy and sell. When this happens, Spirit will guide me to help and correct the problem for many.

CLASS WITH BLUE LIGHTS

October 22, 1980

I am in a classroom. It is surrounded by blue light in force fields. My Aunt Eva (who is dead) was there. I am in charge. Special training is taking place.

My insight: I am receiving special training from Spirit. The room reminded me of the interior of a space ship.

Class With Blue Lights

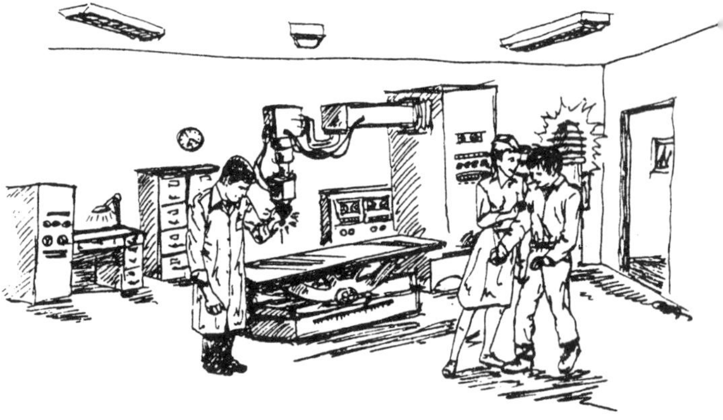

People With Healing Machines

PEOPLE WITH HEALING MACHINES

January 7, 1981

I came into a room where two people were working with healing machines. One of them said, "Good," when he saw me, then told me to lie down so that he could work on me. I thought they were surprised to see me, as if they thought that I wouldn't be able to find them.

My insight: Spirit guides are healing my body for an unknown purpose.

HE IS THE HEART
- THE PUMP -
HE'LL SHOW THE WAY

March 10, 1981

I am talking to some person and suddenly said something about the Christ (or that they still don't understand the Christ) and something about me. Then I pointed my hands and flew into the sky, straight up into the air, right through the trees. I was headed to Virginia from New York, so I thought I would fly 1000 MPH. Then I increased my speed to 3000 MPH so that I could make the trip in 1/3 of an hour. Then I came to this big house. In a corridor I met a group of four or five people. I knew one of them and called him, "Monk." I said, "I came back to the group because Kay Ortman asked me to, but I still don't know what it's all about." Someone said (about me), "He is the Heart-The Pump, so he will show the way to the others." But I still didn't know how.

My insight: I am here to show the way for many people but am not yet aware of how.

KEYS TO THE KINGDOM

March 2, 1982

A voice said, "You shall have the keys to the kingdom."

My insight: My spiritual gifts will enable me to open heaven's gate by serving all mankind. This is another example of a dream that was felt rather than seen and, therefore, hard to put into words.

A PLAY IN A CHURCH

March 16, 1982

I'm in a play in a church. I don't know my part, even with the script right in front of me. I'm to be the king. I'm wondering if I can read my part.

My insight: I will have an important spiritual part to play in life. A common repeated theme is that I don't know exactly what to do, even though the answer is within.

BEINGS MAKE ME INTO A SUPER HERO

August 8, 1984

Some beings are doing a procedure on me, making me into a super hero so that I could serve some helpful purpose.

My insight: I have assistance from the other side helping me to achieve some higher purpose to help mankind.

I'M FROM ANOTHER PLANET

September 14, 1984

I am from another planet. I came to serve all mankind.

My insight: This is not my traditional home. I am here to help souls in this dimension.

SUPER POWERS

January 14, 1985

I have super powers. I make the comment that fighting is not worthy of us.

My insight: I am more that I seem to be on the surface. I have some special abilities (Para Normal). Also, the gift of the spirit should be used for higher purposes (fighting not worthy of us).

FROM ANOTHER WORLD

April 22, 1985

I was a being from another world. A tape telling me how to do things was within and starting to unfold. The information it contained pertained to unlimited energy giving one the ability to travel between worlds.

My insight: I am not what I seem on the surface. I have been programmed to do special things to serve mankind. These programs within are beginning to manifest outwardly.

I'M DIVINELY PROTECTED

August 5, 1985

My brother (Nat) and I are flying. He stops because he is afraid. I say, "Stay with me. As long as you are with me nothing can go wrong, as I am divinely protected and can accomplish my mission in life no matter what it is."

My insight: I am being protected by spirit to fulfill my life's mission.

EARTH IS IN TROUBLE

December 13, 1986

I travel to the future in a large spaceship. Earth is in trouble, so I must go forward in time. When I arrive, someone says, "We've been expecting you."

My insight: I have help from the other side (an unknown source) in order to help mankind in the future. My arrival will be expected.

I CONFRONT EVIL FOR MANY

May 3, 1987

It was predicted that I would confront evil, not just for my self, but for a great many people. Mentally, I put a broken-down bicycle back into shape like new so that I could get back into the race. There was a bully involved. People that I did not know backed me up with a lot of money. I thought there was no way that I could lose because of this backup support. My race number was 7.

My insight: I am here to serve mankind and win a great battle over evil (Bully). With my unseen assistance (Backup Support from the other side, I will be able to carry out my mission. (#7 = perfection)

KNEW ME BETTER THAN I KNEW MYSELF

July 22, 1988

I floated to a place on a slab of concrete. A woman knew me better than I knew myself. I asked about my body condition, injuries, etc., as they were going to help me over these problems.

My insight: Spirit helpers know more about me than I consciously know. They will assist from the other side to heal this body to aid me in carrying out my mission.

TIME TRAVEL

July 10, 1990

I appeared to be in a future Post Atomic war setting. My 1976 Red Buick was in good shape, but surrounded by mud. I cleaned the mud off with energy. Another person had a car like mine, but his was falling apart. I was going to travel back in time to bring something back that would help people. Some man was going to go with me, even though it would be traumatic to relive the atomic war.

My insight: Whether in body or spirit, I will get through the times of upheaval and destruction with strength. Spirit (man) will accompany me.

MISSION FROM COMMANDER

April 30, 1991

There was some type of war setting. I was in the United States. My rank was higher than a captain, but I was not certain exactly what it was. We came up with some idea to win the conflict. It would involve dropping me and my Lieutenant (who worked with me) behind enemy lines. Some large pieces of equipment and machinery would be needed to go with us, and absolute secrecy was essential so that nothing leaked out. We made the comment that all the big officers were walking around looking at each other's medals and decorations and nothing was getting done. Then I went to the headquarters where there was a long line of people waiting in front with some high ranking officers (higher than my rank). As the commander to the chief walked out (I thought he knew me and the mission we were planning) I walked behind him and said, "Can I speak with you, Sir?" I didn't want him to walk away without knowing of the mission. As soon as I mentioned who I was, he said, "Okay; What do you need?" When we got back to their office, he took me in to see the Commander. I told him that I would need to be specially lifted behind enemy lines and given special equipment. So that none of the higher ranking officers would interfere with the operation, I said that I would report only to them, which would mean that I would need a code. I thought of "Lantern" (like Green Lantern) fighting evil everywhere in the name of justice.

My insight: I had a special mission to serve God with heaven's full support. My secret code was "Lantern" (like a super hero).

Psychic Warfare

PSYCHIC WARFARE

August 4, 1991

Something big was happening (Psychic Warfare). I thought I would help out, as I have two powerful angels with me. A lot of powerful beings were on my side, and these people would need it.

My insight: There is a confrontation of good versus evil. I am on heaven's side and have spiritual warriors surrounding me.

SECRET ORGANIZATION KNOWS TRUE IDENTITY

September 15, 1991

I am in a building. There is danger. A secret organization contacts me and is going to help me escape. I ask them, "Do you know enough about me?" They answer, "Yes," and show my name on a screen. It says, "Superman" and lists all my abilities. I am surprised they know that, as I thought it was a secret and nobody knew.

My insight: I am a special soul. Spirit knows all about me and will help when needed.

SPIRIT LED ME

September 24, 1991

I am in an oriental country. A woman recognizes me and calls me by name. I am surprised. She asks what brought me there. I answer, "Spirit led me here. I thought I could do a lecture."

My insight: Spirit will lead me where I need to go.

SETTING RECORDS

December 13, 1991

I was winning and setting new national records. There were people there doing so much for me that I wanted to help also. They were as excited about the outcome as I was.

My insight: Spirit is helping me and is as excited with the outcome as I am.

SUMMONS FROM COMMANDER - IN - CHIEF

July 9, 1992

I was one of the most important chiropractors in the state. I received a summons from the commander-in-chief to drop everything and go do this thing. While I was waiting, I thought that I needed to get a cab but was relieved when I found out that they were providing transportation. They sent a plane with special agents to pick me up and I was going to speak to Superman. They seemed to think very highly of me and had very important work on a special mission for me to do. They said that I was the best for this type of case, and they were going to take me to a place where I could learn some additional information about it.

My insight: I had a mission (call) from God to drop everything and go with some angels who would take me somewhere to learn something that I would need for the mission.

IT WAS PREDICTED

September 2, 1992

I was floating in a body of water and noticed something that looked like a fin in the water. The people around seemed relaxed about it, so I knew it wasn't a shark. They wanted me to grab hold and let it get underneath me so that it could give me a ride. Suddenly I realized I was on the back of an elephant. I was able to drape my arms over it and hang off its back side. It took me up to the shoreline. When we got there, I realized the elephant was huge. It seemed about 50 feet out of the water. It took me to some cliff area where I asked it to put me down. People on the banks were watching, and I began climbing a bank of soft dirt which was difficult to climb, as it was very steep and the dirt would shift. I seemed to know people on top of the cliff. I said, "Isn't it amazing that the elephant gave me a ride here?" Someone answered, "No; although it is rare to see elephants here, it was predicted that an elephant would come

It Was Predicted

and bring someone, but then it would go away. That elephant is not from around here." They obviously thought that I had made the elephant go there. A small child was waiting on me. He was on the ground, and only consisted of a head and neck. He didn't have a body and was very ill. He asked me to take him someplace. He felt that he could wait no longer since he was ill. He said, "It is time" and wanted me to be the one to take him. The setting seemed to be in India.

My insight: My arrival has been anticipated in the physical. It is time to work on the upper aspects of Spirit.

BEINGS FROM ANOTHER GALAXY

August 16, 1992

I was in the back of a van. People took me to a cave-like area in a desert. My usual way of going somewhere was different. They were from another galaxy and were going to do some special maneuver on me and transform me into a super hero. A special train-like car came out of the mountain on wide looking stainless steel tracks. They were removing all their money, stamps, etc. that were on them, as they wouldn't need them where they were going. I wanted some memory of them, but they said they couldn't leave anything behind. They had to destroy everything and even discouraged people from doing a painting or drawing of them.

My insight: Spirit is transforming me to accomplish a higher mission in life to serve all mankind.

I WAS ELVIS

November 4, 1992

I was Elvis Presley. I was with my entourage (about 6 guys) in Mexico, and I was giving money out to the crowds (packs of one and five dollar bills). I was thinking to myself that I couldn't get to everyone, but I did the best I could and had a great time doing it. I was dressed in a very fancy white outfit with sequins. I decided I was ready to leave there because it was getting too crowded, so we headed back to our cars. I threw the keys to one of the guys so that he could drive. Then I sat down in the back seat and rested my head against the shoulder of the person sitting next to me, as I was very tired. Suddenly I noticed a man with a camcorder on the side of the road facing toward the car and wondered if he would catch me in the shadows within the car, as he focused on us while we drove by. The Mexican government had confiscated some electrical equipment from one of my people. They said that he needed papers and wanted to charge him some outrageous amount of money. He let the government people keep it and said he would just get another one in another town. A little later we stopped to eat.

My insight: Once again, I possess special qualities, most of which I'm totally unaware. Also, I will try my best to help all the people I can but will only be able to help so many directly (and will have a great time doing it).

Chapter Six

UNUSUAL DREAMS

INTRODUCTION

The dreams found in this chapter are exactly what the title states, very unusual. Whether I find myself in an elevator with God in these dreams or am being introduced as the next president, they are all strangely unique.

Why do we have dreams of this nature? I feel that the answer to that lies within the individual's subconscious mind. We have all pictured ourselves doing things that we would never have the nerve to act out in reality. This is how the subconscious mind differs from the conscious mind. It dares to do anything, go anywhere or wear anybody's shoes. It likes to ask questions like: "I wonder what it would be like to do this or that, or feel this or that?"

I like my unusual dreams. They allow me to talk with movie stars (even those deceased), travel to other worlds (space station) and even become the President.

DIDN'T WANT TO GO ON

December 17, 1980

I was fighting with two people with guns. There was a lot of bloodshed, but they kept coming for more. Finally I said I couldn't stand it anymore. So I drove my car through a huge super market window. As I crashed through the glass, I grabbed a piece of glass and cut my throat on the jugular area to make certain I would die, as I didn't want to go on. I was still conscious afterward, although I felt like I was floating. My friend, Ralph, found me lying there. I looked a fright, but he was very calm, checking to see if I was still breathing and alive (which I was). Then other spirits that I knew came (Dr. McGarey; Rosalyn Bruyere; and one of my patients that I knew in Spirit). First they checked to see if my physical body was still connected to my astral body. Then they assisted in my healing process because I still had something important I needed to do. I was bandaged up and weak and was going to give a speech with Olga Worrell. I asked who was taking care of my store (I had a supermarket) and clinic. They said that they had put up a sign saying, "Closed due to cold weather," and it was accepted without question. They weren't covering my business for me but told me that it would be all right until I got well.

My insight: No matter how discouraged I may get, Spirit is there encouraging and nudging me on, reminding me of the important work I have to do until my time is up.

I'M NOT DR. SAUL SHAYE

January 28, 1981

A girl I knew was taking me to visit her folks (though they didn't look the same). She was engaged to someone else (a doctor) yet she brought me to their house and introduced me as that person. I was hoping they wouldn't ask me questions that that doctor knew, like how it was growing up in a Jewish home living in Brooklyn, etc. She introduced me as Dr. Shaye, but I knew in the dream that I wasn't he.

My insight: The dream seemed to hint at the possibility that I just might be a walk-in soul and not the original "Saul Shaye" who grew up in Brooklyn.

I GIVE SERMON

August 15, 1984

I am in a church in England. The head person is intoxicated so they ask me to read. First, I ask for a moment of silence, but someone interrupts and asks to postpone the service. I back away but then decide I am going to give a sermon-type speech and do just that. I proceed to present this moving, powerful sermon to the church, but afterwards, I don't want to talk to anyone, so I lift up and fly in an upright position down the steps and start flying over the people.

My insight: I want to help and inspire people but want to avoid intellectualizing the material.

REAGAN INTRODUCES THE PRESIDENT

January 4, 1985

I was talking with President Reagan about the future of mankind and the planet. We seemed to be in total agreement. After awhile, I took off and flew with some golden shining particles that were in a stream and were like souls of people. After I decided to land, President Reagan addressed a crowd of people. He said to them, "Let me introduce the Vice President' and introduced someone. Then he said, "Now let me introduce the President, Saul Shaye."

My insight: Spirit has some great expectations of me.

RIGHTEOUS INDIGNATION

June 28, 1985

I was in a lecture hall in front of an audience, when I saw some people holding knives threatening the people around them, as though they were extorting something from them. I said, "What do you think you're doing?" Then I ran up to one of them, and he got so scared that he dropped his weapon, and there was a scuffle with the people around him. As I walked back to the front, someone said, "That was an amazing thing you just did." I said, "When something seems right, I forget about danger and just charge with righteous indignation and with no thought of danger." Then I started telling the audience of some dreams I have had with symbols of my becoming president (like the one Reagan announces me, "and now your next president, Saul Shaye). Someone said, "You'll know someone by how much opposition he generates." It was time to close, but my brother wanted me to finish telling my stories about my beingpresident.

My insight: Spirit is reminding me of its expectations but also letting me know that, when something is right, do what needs to be done knowing that they are behind me.

A VERY UNUSUAL HEALING

August 21, 1986

I did a weird procedure on a woman I knew at Findhorn who was in a wheelchair. I cut off the bottom of her foot. Then I decided that it wasn't cut off high enough so I cut off more. I took this big knife and cut off large slices until I had cut it off almost to the knee. I then tied it with a big towel. Then she put on her shoe right over the stump. Then I did the same procedure on the opposite leg. Then I asked her if she would need some special assistance to get onto her crutches. She said," No." I said," I don't understand " (as she didn't have any legs from the knees down). She was in a real praising mood saying, "Thank you so much and thank God." It seemed like she was able to walk right away. Then it seemed like her heart was acting up. I had to do open-heart surgery. I cut right in, even though I didn't have any idea what I was doing, but the Spirit was moving me. I finished and got her relaxed, and everything was okay. Then I'm crying, and I'm real emotional. I say, "I don't understand this procedure at all. You really have to have tremendous faith to go ahead with things like this because it's so much more than what we know". Then I told the woman what was done. She said, "That's totally amazing." She was now totally well and didn't know this was done but she is fine now. I said, 'That's great." I was so happy for her. Then I was in some doctor's setting, and I was walking around these people. All of a sudden I said, "This has to be cut open right now or this person will die." A doctor said, "What do you mean?" I just cut the person open and said, "See what I mean." I show the doctor some embolism that was going to rupture. I said "All I can say is I can see right into the people, so I know I have to act on it immediately." The other doctors thought I should become a full doctor because of the ability I had.

FOOTNOTE: As I was chopping off the woman's legs, the tissues were regenerating immediately. It was scary to have the responsibility to do this procedure even though it was healing right away.

My insight: Much of the healing, that will be done through me, will be done without my conscious awareness. I will have to "Let go and Let God."

SPACE STATION

August 24, 1986

A gigantic building was going to be constructed, which was very sensitive to vibrations and atomic bombs. To build it, missiles were to be sent up with people to build portions of it in outer space. I'm up on what seems to be a clinic on the space platform with a couple of older matronly-like women and about two other doctors. "Isn't this exciting," I said. "Here we are in outer space, almost as comfortable as home." All of a sudden we received an urgent message about our weight being too heavy, which would threaten the space station. With no hesitation, one of the men opened a door and stepped out, which should have been instant death. (I was the man). But instead of finding myself in a black void of space, I found myself outside of a house surrounded by grass with a lot of flowers. I said, "This is weird." It felt like a (twilight zone) story. I went back into the ship. One of the other doctors is looking quite shocked to see me okay again. I said, "I need to show you something, if you have the nerve to follow me." He does, and we step out of the space ship. It is the same setting that I had observed a few moments before (a house surrounded by a large green field with flowers). He looked at this hill behind us and said, "That looks like someplace I once dreamed of or dreamt of building." Next to our house was another house off to the left with people sitting outside on benches. I said, "Are they real or is this all imagination?" We walked up to these people who seemed black. Next, the doctor introduced us to the people. They formed a line and, when the others were introduced, they gave the person a long hug. At the end of the line was a tall woman with long blond hair. The woman turned to me, and my friend hesitated with my name. I said, "Shaye," and we embraced. The woman was wearing a low-cut gown or dress, and my head came up only to her neck line, So my face was pressed against her breasts. She held the position, and it was very warm and nurturing (not sexual, but heart moving).

My insight: No greater love hath he who would give his life for that of his brother. Instead of death, a paradise situation seemed to open after the decision to sacrifice self for the survival of others. The black people with the tall blond person reminds me of UFO symbols with the tall blond person being somewhat angelic.

MICHAEL LANDON AND ME — ONE OVERSOUL

February 13, 1987

I was talking to Michael Landon and his parents about how many similarities we had as children. Michael Landon asked me if I believed in Jesusism. I said, "Jesusism? Do you mean belief in Jesus and what he stood for? If so, I do now; I didn't then." It seemed that he was very much into Judaism. Then there was the thought that if his soul and mine could be combined as one with each of our strong points, what a powerful, dedicated over-soul that would make.

My insight: "Where two or more are gathered in my name, there will I be also." If two souls could share joint purpose in Christ, they would make a very strong union.

DREAM MAN

June 26, 1990

I was asked if I was the Dream Man. I answered, "Yes. Dreams changed by life. I went from an atheist to a healer and believer and other things." I got choked up emotionally talking about it.

My insight: I have been given the gift of dreaming.

SECRET PASSAGE TO TIBET

1990

A mythical creature, half man and half beast, shows me a special entrance way into a large tree trunk. His legs are like those of an elephant with large nails on the side. I go in and come to a rope bridge that extends over a very deep chasm that's quite frightening due to its height. There is a pair of work overalls extending from the end of the bridge. I want to continue on the path, so I have to extend my body and stretch out until I can slip into the overalls. When I do this, the overalls release from the end of the rope bridge and another pair appears in its place. I follow a secret passageway until I come to a sign that reads, "Welcome to Tibet." Then I am met by three lamas sitting with legs crossed. They present me with a beautiful lotus and tell me to go to a room, and they will meet me later in my dreams.

My insight: A magical way is being shown to me, but I have to dare to extend myself and reach for the path and do the work. This path is open for others to follow (another pair of overalls took its place). If I do this, secrets (gifts - The Lotus) will be explained to me in my dreams.

COULD SEE BACK IN TIME

July 14, 1991

I took a magnifying glass to look at some dots. Then I took a camera to take pictures. I saw my brother, Norman, and his wife, Maddy, and their son, David. David looked to be about six years old. There were some very shiny cars in front of them, but they were old models. I looked off to the side, and Saul and Shari were standing there. In the dream, I asked, "How can we be seeing ourselves unless we are looking back in time." I saw an apartment with my old brown 1970 Buick Electra in front of it.

My insight: First and only time I saw myself in a dream as another body or two separate beings. I don't know what this dream meant, but it was very unusual to be able to see myself like that.

IN AN ELEVATOR WITH GOD

October 28, 1991

I am in an elevator with God (who looks like George Burns). The elevator is moving, bouncing around like it's flying. I'm so excited knowing who I'm talking to that I want to make sure I remember everything in the dream (knew I was dreaming). I wanted to be certain I would get the whole conversation written down. I said, "If you are God, what is it all about?" He answers, "It's about what you think it's about. Life goes on." I was worrying so much about getting the answers that I didn't take full advantage of my being there talking to Him. Before I knew it, He said, "Okay. You just do what you can," and then He was gone.

My insight: It is difficult to express Spirit in words. One must experience it with one's heart. I try to analyze things too much mentally rather than just feel them.

FINDHORN WAS SURROUNDED

I was driving an eighteen wheeler heading towards Findhorn. They were in danger and were surrounded by enemy soldiers. I appeared in a room in the midst of the conflict and was filled with the Holy Spirit. I pointed a finger at the enemy soldiers, and, one at a time, I said, "Be Gone," and de-materialized them through the walls until the only one left was the enemy general. I looked into his heart and said, "It's okay. You can stay."

My insight: When the Findhorn Community will have serious problems, I will be greatly empowered to help them overcome their adversaries.

SPIRITUAL HEALERS AERIAL HIGHWAY

April 5, 1992

A huge new highway was built, called "The spiritual healers aerial highway." It was up in the sky like a space age movie. I was walking at an extremely fast pace, weaving around people on a road that was by a body of water. Suddenly, the road came to a point where it started going so steeply uphill that it wasn't possible to walk anymore, so I went inside to pay some money in order to get on the highway. Then I went to platform #6, which was extremely crowded with students and somewhat like an airport. The train, that I wanted, had already left, so I just waited there. I spotted some people (who appeared to be oriental) bothering a woman. I went out of my way to see what was happening. As I came around the corner, a gang started walking up to me. One of the husky looking orientals said to me, "Who are you looking at?" We began to fight, and I beat him up badly with a punch to the face, followed by a punch to the body. None of the others bothered me when they saw him fall down. Afterward, I started talking to the guys and said, "He is a fairly good fighter but needs work on some things." Then I helped the guy up. I started telling them how he could improve his techniques, and they were very interested. "His combinations are good," I said, "But he needs work on other moves." The oriental that I beat up told me that he studied some karate. [It felt good to be in control but also felt good that my actions were magnanimous after winning the fight, instead of rubbing it in to them that I had won. I, also, realized that he was no real threat to me, but, without fighting, I couldn't have won them over. I also told them that I was a chiropractor.]

My insight: The Spiritual Healers Association will be a great organization in the future, but it will take work to establish it and win over the opposition.

CLINTON HIGH SCHOOL-
COACH MOSES

1994

I was in a school. I had only one major subject to complete and a few minor ones. It was Clinton High School and was going to be under the guidance of Coach Moses.

My insight: During the years of President Clinton's presidency I would be finishing up my preparation for my life's task, with Spirit guiding me until it's done.

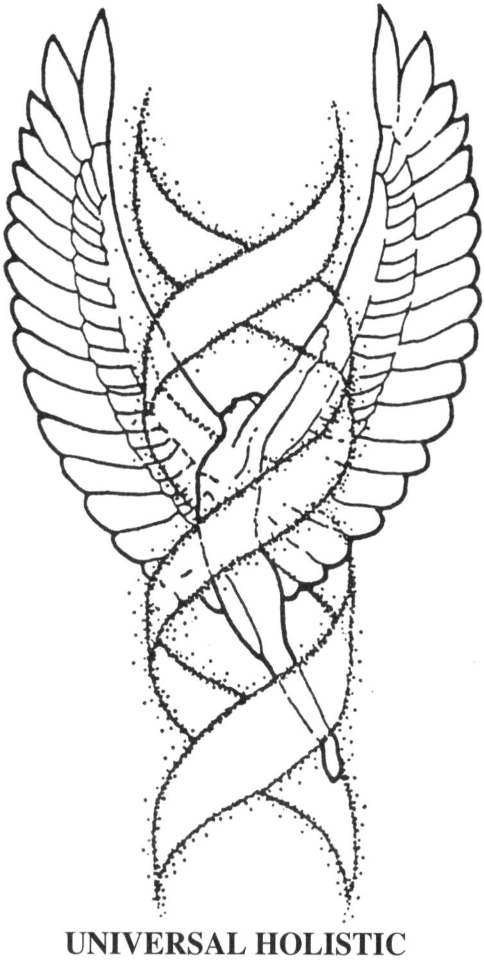

UNIVERSAL HOLISTIC HEALERS ASSOCIATION
MT. PLEASANT, SC 29445
(1990-1999)

Chapter Seven

MY PERSONAL KEYS TO BETTER DREAM RECALL

There is one question I have been asked repeatedly through the years, and that is: "How do you remember so many dreams in vivid detail as often as you do?" After pondering the question, I came up with the following list of my own personal necessary perimeters that I have come to associate with good dream recall. Although it is true that I have had some first-rate dreams in unfavorable situations, my best dream recall occurs when the following conditions exist. You may or may not require all of these, but, for one to have exceptional remembrance of dreams, it is important to pay attention to the circumstances that are favorable to one's own dream recall.

1. ATMOSPHERE: My ideal atmosphere is a room that enables me to go into a deep, hibernation-type sleep in a very short period of time. It must be cool to cold, which for me is 66 to 68 degrees (F.). All light from windows must be blocked out (even around doors) if the nap is during the day. A small night light, twenty or more feet away from me is the most light I can tolerate without disturbance. In other words, a cold, darkened room.

2. PHYSICAL REQUIREMENTS: Ideally, I shouldn't be exhausted. When I'm very tired, I go into a deep sleep and don't wake up until I'm rested, which may be morning. I need at least seven hours sleep per night, with at least a one hour nap during the day for optimal relaxation. Food is, also, important. It is best not to eat heavily right before bedtime. If you're hungry, fruit seems to be the easiest on digestion, which enables one to sleep for optimal dream recall. A heavy meal at bedtime is the same as being exhausted.

3. EMOTIONAL REQUIREMENTS: It is best to be emotionally relaxed and at peace close to bedtime (meaning, don't have any unresolved strong emotions that you will take to bed with you.) Otherwise, your night may just be tossing and turning in a fitful sleep. Arguments at bedtime are a good way for the subconscious to produce a fear dream or nightmare. Five or ten minutes of quiet time (meditation) right before sleep prepares the subconscious for better communication with spirit.

4. SPIRITUAL REQUIREMENTS: Meditation applies here, also, as it attunes the physical and emotional body to its true state (which is Spirit). Prayer time before going to sleep is helpful in removing self and turning one's life over to a higher source, which opens the subconscious to more guidance. A clear conscience is helpful, as far as how one is living one's life based on his/her personal spiritual concepts. (If, in your culture, showing one's face is immoral, don't do it). You need to be at peace with what you consider very important living criteria. If you know that stealing is wrong but do it anyway, your conscience is not at peace. All we are required to do is what we know to do.

5. SOCIAL REQUIREMENTS: For me it is best to sleep in a room alone so that there are no distractions or hesitations in my mind on waking up, making sounds or saying anything (X-rated material or comments about another person or even comments about yourself that you may not want anyone to hear). The subconscious translates any hesitation or awkwardness as a signal to forget the dream.

6. REINFORCEMENT: It is very important that dreams should be written out and said out loud to others. Most meaningful dreams could be placed in a conspicuous area where you can visually reinforce the important aspects of it. Recording is the way to get the most recall possible, but writing the dream out and seeing it will reinforce the message.

7. RECORDING REQUIREMENT: The less movement and thinking one does upon awaking, the better. It is for this reason that I have a cassette recorder next to my bed (Always in the same place, which for me is on the right) with a hand held microphone. I keep the recorder on "record" and the mike on "off." This way, when I wake up, all I have to do is move my right hand, pick up the mike and flick the switch. Then, lying back down with my eyes closed, I record everything I remember. It is very important to list every detail, even if it is embarrassing or seemingly insignificant, for little details can stimulate further memory. It is my belief that we have to show our subconscious that we are willing to make the effort. The more willingness we demonstrate, the more that is given.

8. GET THE SENSES INVOLVED: Use the five senses as much as possible to reinforce the dream content. By writing it out, you can see the dream; by talking about the dream to others, you can hear and speak it; to feel the dream, visualize the experience until you are reliving it. All of this reinforces the memory. If there was a sense of smell in the dream, duplicating a similar odor may reinforce the dream memory. Physically, I have acted out parts of my dreams in my lectures, which reinforces my memories.

CONCLUSION

I have tried to instill in the reader some of the excitement and inspiration I initially experienced when I read, There Is A River, which was further reinforced after I attended my first A.R.E. Holistic Health Conference in Phoenix, Arizona, in 1976. Drs. William and Gladys McGarey and Dr. Herb Puryear were so enthusiastic about dreams and gave the topic such a rousing endorsement that I left the conference with a heightened determination to learn more about my dreams and began to delve more deeply into this untapped source of information.

These one hundred (or so) dreams are meant to show the reader how practical information, spiritual insight and even glimpses into the future can be received through one's own dreams. Dreams are a way for one to be more than a body and a personal ego; they can be a gateway to Spirit and, thus, can tremendously enhance our lives. It is difficult to describe the enjoyment I have received at those times that I have left my physical body behind, and entered that euphoric, amazing and enticing "other" world of dreams. It is almost embarrassing to admit that there are times that I can hardly wait to go to sleep, day or night, to see what adventure awaits me there.

Whether my subconscious takes me on a safari, into a spaceship or to heaven itself, those dreams are memories as strong as anything I've ever done physically. I've even had numerous dreams about previous dreams. Whether we do something physically while awake or mentally while asleep in a dream state, the subconscious remembers both equally (if the dreams are reinforced).

The dreams I've shared with you in this book are just a fraction of the dreams I've had in the last seventeen years. I must admit that it was difficult to pick and choose what to leave in and what to leave out, as so many of my dreams are, what I consider, great dreams. Toward the end of the book, it seemed that I'd wake up every morning with at least one more dream I wanted to add but finally said, "Enough," and ended the book, even though my dreams were, and still are, flowing with messages from beyond.

Join me on my spiritual quest for greater awareness and awaken your own "Dream Man" within. Everyone has a special gift, so whether you are a teacher, a healer or a dreamer, your gift is very important. We all have a mission in life of one kind or another, and no one purpose is greater or more important than any other. God sent us to earth for many reasons and many missions. As for me, I'll keep "walking on two worlds."

COMMENTS ABOUT WORKSHOPS, AND HEALING SESSIONS

"Your Sunday lesson was inspiring. Your workshop impressive. The feedback from those who had private sessions with you has been overwhelmingly positive. Many people felt significant results and some described their experience after the session as "miraculous". We are all looking forward to your next visit with us"

Unity Church of Memphis
Connie Freeman, Minister
Memphis, Tennessee

"You are the genuine article and truly work to share your remakable gift with all the people. With clear conscience, I can highly recommend you and your work."

Unity Church of Ocala
J. Scott Thornton, Minister
Ocala, Florida

"Everyone who had a healing session with you has very positive comments about your professional manner and sincere devotion to their well being. Some people have spoken of very definite healings after being with you. I wholeheartedly enjoyed having you here and enthusiastically recommend your visit to any church or spiritual organization."

First Church of Religious Science
Rev. Patrick Rolland
Albuquerque, New Mexico

COMMENTS ABOUT WORKSHOPS

"The best workshop we've ever had... exact quote from many of our attendees..."

Unity Church of the Hill Country
Re. John McKee
Kerrville, Texas

"It has been a truly great blessing having you here in our church. Your energy is beautiful, very clear and your intengrity, impeccable. Your example speaks even louder than your words."

Unity Church For Love & Light
Rev. Carolyn Wenzel
Friendswood, Texas

"What a gift you shared with our Unity Ministry for the past few days. The feedback has been glowing..."

Unity Center for Positive Living
Rev. Ann Marie Acacio
Wilkes-Barre, PA

"Your workshop was a wonderful, practical, healing and very enlightening experience"

Unity Church of Charleston
Rev. Mary Ann Finch
Charleston, SC

"It is encouraging to see someone with such rich spiritual gifts share them so willingly and give credit to God, where credit belongs."

Unity Church of Harrisburg
Rev. Claudell Hefner
Mechanicsburg, PA

"You presented extraordinary material in a very down to earth, non-patronizing manner."

Unity Church of Dallas
Director of Special Events

"...extraordinary lessons, insights and constructive methods toward healing, mind, body, and spirit."

Unity Church of Christianity
Rev. Ken Murdock
Ft. Myers, FL

"What a blessing you brought to Tampa Unity...the workshop... the private healing sessions...all proved to be so beneficial."

Tampa Unity
Rev. Ross Goodman
Tampa, FL

"Thank you for the professional, enlightening, and down-to-earth workshop on healing. The workshop was gratifying and financial rewarding to my church."

Unity Church of Vermont
Pat Carpenter

"...fascinating story of a healer..."

Unity of Naples Church
Rev. Jack Kern
Naples, Florida